3.9
.5
t 119611

OTTERS

Sara Swan Miller

PowerKiDS press
New York

For Chris
Play, play, play!

Published in 2008 by The Rosen Publishing Group, Inc.
29 East 21st Street, New York, NY 10010

Copyright © 2008 by The Rosen Publishing Group, Inc.

All rights reserved. No part of this book may be reproduced in any form without permission in writing from the publisher, except by a reviewer.

First Edition

Editor: Amelie von Zumbusch
Book Design: Julio Gil
Photo Researcher: Nicole Pristash

Photo Credits: Cover, pp. 5, 7, 15, 21 Shutterstock.com; p. 9 © istockphoto.com/Jan Gottwald; p. 11 © istockphoto.com/Roger Sieber; p. 13 © istockphoto.com/Darren Hunt; p. 17 © Getty Images; p. 19 © Jeff Foott/Getty Images.

Library of Congress Cataloging-in-Publication Data

Miller, Sara Swan.
  Otters / Sara Swan Miller. — 1st ed.
      p. cm. — (Paws and claws)
  Includes index.
  ISBN 978-1-4042-4162-6 (library binding)
  1. Otters—Juvenile literature. I. Title.
  QL737.C25M555 2008
  599.769—dc22
                                                    2007018506

Manufactured in the United States of America

Contents

Playful Otters	4
Skilled Swimmers	6
Otter Paws and Claws	8
Water Acrobats	10
Dinnertime!	12
Play, Play, Play!	14
River Otter Pups	16
Sea Otter Babies	18
Danger!	20
Can Otters Be Saved?	22
Glossary	23
Index	24
Web Sites	24

Playful Otters

Otters love to play! These **mammals** can live in almost all parts of the world, as long as there is water in which they can play and hunt. There are 13 different **species** of otters. All otters spend most of their time in the water.

The main groups of otters are river otters, sea otters, and giant otters. River otters live in North America, South America, Europe, Asia, and Africa. Sea otters live along the coasts of the Pacific Ocean. Giant otters live only in South America. Most otters are small, but giant otters can grow to 6 feet (1.8 m) long!

North American river otters, like these two, are also called northern river otters. They live in Canada and the United States.

Skilled Swimmers

Otters are perfectly suited for life in the water. They can swim easily by moving their long, thin body up and down. Otters breathe air, so they have to come up from time to time to catch a breath. When an otter dives, its nose and ears close up to keep out the water. Some otters can stay underwater for up to 8 minutes!

Otters have thick, brown fur that keeps them warm. The long hairs on the outside of an otter's coat make it waterproof. The soft fur underneath traps warm air next to its body.

Otters can stay underwater for several minutes. Then, they need to come up to breathe air.

Otter Paws and Claws

An otter's paws and claws are well suited to life in the water, too. Otters have short, strong legs to help push them along. Otters generally have webbed feet, like ducks. These feet act like oars. Most otters have long, sharp claws. These claws are very useful for holding the slippery fish that otters catch. Not all otters have sharp claws, though. Two species in Africa have no claws at all.

Otters can move easily on land, too. They bound along on their strong legs with their back **arched**. When they can, otters drop down and slide on mud.

While otters sometimes stand up on their back legs to take a look around, they generally walk on all four legs.

Water Acrobats

    Otters are excellent swimmers. They push themselves through the water by moving their body up and down. They wave their webbed back feet to go even faster. Their long, strong tail swings back and forth behind them.

    In the water, otters are real **acrobats**. They twist and turn and dive. Sometimes they slide quickly just under the surface. They even do somersaults! At times, otters swim on their side or on their back. Every so often, an otter will take a rest and just float on top of the water. That never lasts long, though. Otters cannot seem to stay still!

Some otters even nap in the water! Sea otters often hold hands while they sleep so that they do not drift apart.

Dinnertime!

All otters are **carnivores**. This means they eat meat. River otters often live in groups, but they hunt alone. Mostly, they catch water animals. Fish are their favorite, but they also like **crayfish**, frogs, and bugs. Otters have long **whiskers** that help them feel their **prey** in muddy water. On land, river otters may hunt small mammals and even birds. Sea otters eat sea animals they find near the shore, such as crabs, clams, snails, sea urchins, and mussels.

Otters are hunters, but they are also hunted. Eagles, bears, **coyotes**, and killer whales are just some of their enemies.

Otters often hold their prey with their claws while biting off pieces of meat with their sharp teeth.

Play, Play, Play!

Otters are some of the most playful animals you will ever see. When an otter is not hunting or sleeping, it is generally playing.

Otters love to play with each other. They chase each other underwater. They jump on each other and **wrestle** until one gives up. On land, otters love to slide on mud or ice. They will slide down a muddy hill into the water over and over. Otters also think it is fun to push sticks and leaves along the top of the water. Diving for small stones is lots of fun, too.

This playful otter is hiding in a hole in a log. Otters also play hide-and-seek in tall grasses and in the snow.

River Otter Pups

When a mother river otter is about to have pups, she knows she needs a den for them. River otter dens are generally in a riverbank. They have a tunnel that opens underwater and leads up to a nest room. The mother lines the den with soft hair, grass, and moss.

One to six sightless, helpless pups are born at a time. They finally open their eyes when they are a month old. Now it is time for them to learn to swim. Their mother pushes the pups into the water. Soon they are swimming and playing like adult otters.

This young otter is an Asian short-clawed otter. This kind of otter often has a litter, or group, of pups twice a year.

Sea Otter Babies

Sea otters spend most of their time in the ocean. They even give birth in the water. A mother sea otter generally has just one pup at a time. When she has given birth, a sea otter mother lies on her back and holds her helpless baby on her chest.

Pups drink their mother's milk. When a pup is a little older, its mother may cover it in seaweed to keep it safe while she hunts. Once the pup is ready to eat its own food, its mother teaches it how to open a clam by banging it with a stone.

Sea otter pups generally stay with their mother for about six months before going off on their own.

Danger!

There were once plenty of otters living all over the world. Now there are very few. Many species of otters are **endangered**, which means that they may disappear forever. One danger for otters is that people kill them for their skins. Otter skins are very soft and warm. People who sell them can make lots of money.

Another problem for otters is oil spills. Otters need their fur to keep them warm. Fur coated in oil cannot keep an otter warm, and it may die. When otters try to clean their fur, they often swallow oil. This can also kill an otter.

Most water mammals have extra fat to keep them warm, but sea otters count on their fur. They must keep their fur very clean.

Can Otters Be Saved?

Some people are trying to help otters. People have made rules to try to keep oil spills from happening. In many places, people have made it against the law to kill otters. However, there are still some people who break the law.

People are bringing otters back to some places where they used to live. River otters have been brought back to the Hudson River, for example. Hopefully, these otters will make a comeback and romp in the river once more. That way, people will be able to watch and learn about these water acrobats for many years to come.

Glossary

acrobats (A-kruh-bats) Those who have good control of their body and can jump, flip over, and change positions quickly.

arched (ARCHD) Bent over in the shape of a half circle.

carnivores (KAHR-neh-vorz) Animals that eat other animals.

coyotes (ky-OH-teez) Animals that live in North America and look like small, thin wolves.

crayfish (KRAY-fish) Animals with a hard outside and claws that live in freshwater.

endangered (in-DAYN-jerd) In danger of no longer living.

mammals (MA-mulz) Warm-blooded animals that have a backbone and hair, breathe air, and feed milk to their young.

prey (PRAY) An animal that is hunted by another animal for food.

species (SPEE-sheez) One kind of living thing. All people are one species.

whiskers (HWIS-kerz) Hard hairs that grow on a face.

wrestle (REH-sul) To try to force another person or animal to the ground.

Index

A
Africa, 4, 8

B
body, 6, 10
breath, 6

C
carnivores, 12
coyotes, 12
crayfish, 12

E
ears, 6
Europe, 4

F
fur, 6, 20

H
hair(s), 6, 16

L
legs, 8

M
mammals, 4, 12

N
North America, 4
nose, 6

P
Pacific Ocean, 4
prey, 12

S
South America, 4
species, 4, 8, 20

W
water, 4, 6, 8, 10, 12, 14, 16, 18
whiskers, 12

Web Sites

Due to the changing nature of Internet links, PowerKids Press has developed an online list of Web sites related to the subject of this book. This site is updated regularly. Please use this link to access the list:
www.powerkidslinks.com/paws/otters/